The Family Bedtime
TREASURY
TALES for SLEEPY TIMES and SWEET DREAMS

Houghton Mifflin Harcourt
Boston New York 2012

Bedtime is a magical part of a child's world . . .

What makes for a perfect bedtime? Cozy pajamas, comforting music, sharing just the right story or poems with someone you love. You provide the pajamas, and *The Family Bedtime Treasury* will provide the rest! Collected in this treasury are classic bedtime stories and new favorites, as well as poems from Joyce Sidman, Calef Brown, Maxine Kumin, and many more— each ideal to share at naptime or bedtime. So open the pages of this treasury to discover the stories and poems you need to send your one little off to happy dreams.

Contents

The Napping House

Audrey Wood   Don Wood

For Maegerine Thompson Brewer

There is a house,
a napping house,
where everyone is sleeping.

And in that house
there is a bed,
a cozy bed
in a napping house,
where everyone is sleeping.

And on that bed
there is a granny,
a snoring granny
on a cozy bed
in a napping house,
where everyone is sleeping.

And on that granny
there is a child,
a dreaming child
on a snoring granny
on a cozy bed
in a napping house,
where everyone is sleeping.

And on that child
there is a dog,
a dozing dog
on a dreaming child
on a snoring granny
on a cozy bed
in a napping house,
where everyone is sleeping.

And on that dog
there is a cat,
a snoozing cat
on a dozing dog
on a dreaming child
on a snoring granny
on a cozy bed
in a napping house,
where everyone is sleeping.

14

And on that cat
there is a mouse,
a slumbering mouse
on a snoozing cat
on a dozing dog
on a dreaming child
on a snoring granny
on a cozy bed
in a napping house,
where everyone is sleeping.

And on that mouse
there is a flea. . . .

Can it be?
A wakeful flea
on a slumbering mouse
on a snoozing cat
on a dozing dog
on a dreaming child
on a snoring granny
on a cozy bed
in a napping house,
where everyone is sleeping.

A wakeful flea
who bites the mouse,

20

who scares the cat,

who claws the dog,

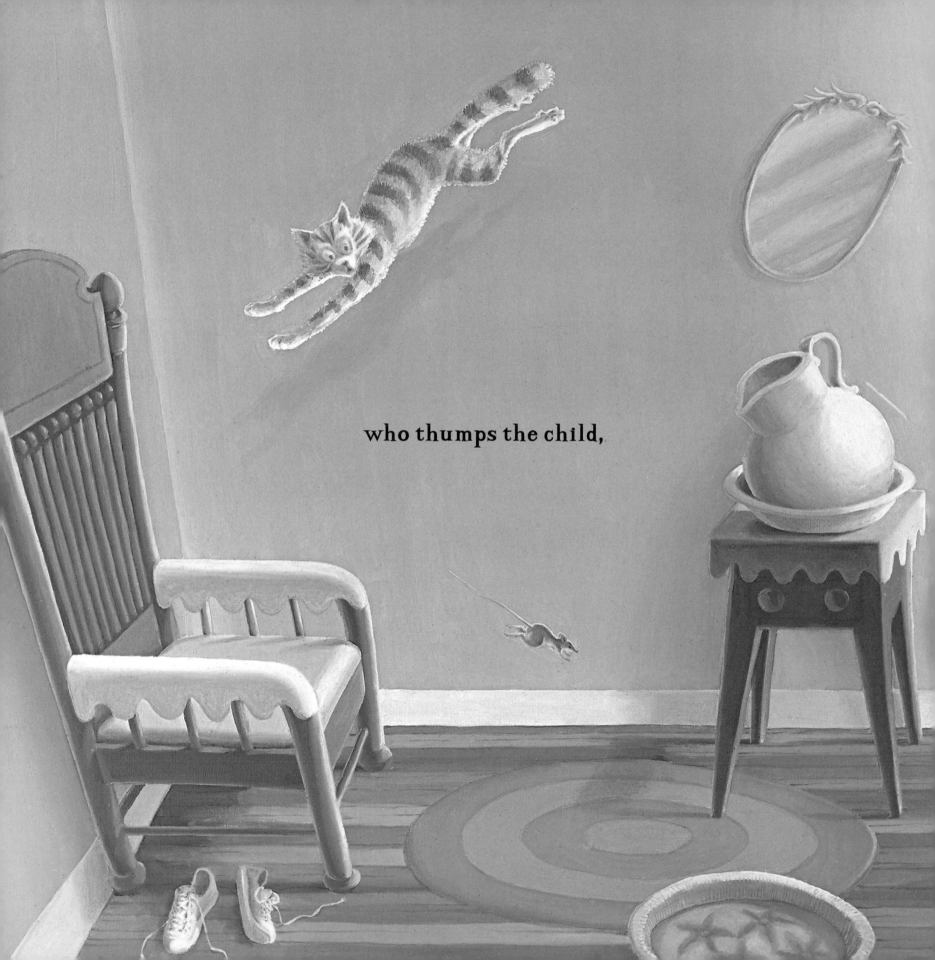

who thumps the child,

who bumps the granny,

who breaks the bed,

in the napping house,
where no one now is sleeping.

Welcome to the Night

To all of you who crawl and creep,
who buzz and chirp and hoot and peep,
who wake at dusk and throw off sleep:
Welcome to the night.

To you who make the forest sing,
who dip and dodge on silent wing,
who flutter, hover, clasp, and cling:
Welcome to the night!

Come feel the cool and shadowed breeze,
come smell your way among the trees,
come touch rough bark and leathered leaves:
Welcome to the night.

The night's a sea of dappled dark,
the night's a feast of sound and spark,
the night's a wild, enchanted park.
Welcome to the night!

As night falls, the nocturnal world wakes. Mice begin to stir, moths flutter into the starlight, and deer step out from hidden places to roam and forage. Having rested all day in a hollow tree, the **raccoon** lumbers down at dusk to search for food. Curious, intelligent, and omnivorous, the raccoon has nimble front paws that are good for digging, climbing, and prying open almost anything. Its well-developed sense of touch—almost unparalleled in the mammal world—serves it well in the darkness. Making its unhurried way across the forest, the raccoon forages by feel— inside a log (for insects), down a hole (for eggs), even underwater (for frogs or crayfish).

by Joyce Sidman
illustrated by Rick Allen

For the latest batch of monkeys:
Hazel, Leo, and Nola May

WHEN the five little monkeys are ready for bed,
their Mama reads stories, then kisses each head.

"It's bedtime for monkeys! Now turn out the light."
"Oh, Mama! Oh, PLEASE! One more story tonight!"

But Mama's too tired. She's read more than four.
"Lights out! Sweet dreams!" She closes their door.

One monkey whispers, "This book looks so good!
If Mama won't read it, then maybe we could."

Then out come the tissues. They ALL start to bawl.
They sob and they cry till the last page of all.

It's such a good ending, their sobs turn to cheers.
Those monkeys are LOUD! (You should cover your ears!)

In fact, they're so noisy that Mama runs in.
"What's all this racket? This chaos? This din?"

One monkey admits with a guilt-ridden look,
"We've been reading the very best, happy, sad book!"

Mama raises an eyebrow. "What was it I said?"

Then one monkey sighs as she turns out the light.
"I wish we could read this new ghost book tonight."

"Just look at that goblin and mean-looking ghost!"
"It's those shadowy bats that I like the most."

HOOO-o

One monkey starts hooting—an eerie ghost sound.
And soon they're all wailing and jumping around!

Then a dark, spooky shadow appears on the wall.
But a knock on their door is what frightens them ALL!

53

. . . Mama walks in!
"What's all this racket?
This chaos? This din?"

The monkeys all gasp. "We thought YOU were the ghost!

This book is so scary. We like it the most!"

Mama raises an eyebrow. "What was it I said?"

One monkey shivers. "That book was so creepy,
so GOOD but so scary, I'll never be sleepy!"

She pulls out a joke book. "We've got to be quiet."
But the jokes are so funny! In fact, they're a riot!

The monkeys try hard not to giggle or laugh.
But then there's a joke with a foolish giraffe.

It's so silly, so goofy, they all start to roar!
And then can you guess who flings open their door?

Oh, yes! It's Mama! She comes storming right in.
"What's all this racket? This chaos? This din?"

The monkeys keep giggling. They JUST cannot quit!
Mama picks up their books. "I've had it! That's it!"
Then she raises an eyebrow. "Did you hear what I said?"

Well, the monkeys are tired. They're almost asleep
when they hear someone giggle, then laugh, and then weep.

"Do you hear all that noise? And just WHO can it BE?"
"Let's sneak down the hall." (Can you guess what they see?)

"Oh, Mama!" they giggle. "What was it you said?"

Those monkeys are sleepy! They head out the door.
"Just wait till tomorrow, and then we'll read more!"

Curious Dreamer,
**WILL YOU SWIM
THROUGH THE SEA?
AND DIVE AMONG
DOLPHINS AND FISHES
WITH GLEE?**

 *Curious Dreamer,*
**SNUGGLE IN TIGHT. WHAT DO
YOU THINK YOU WILL DREAM
OF TONIGHT?**

 Curious Dreamer,
**WILL YOU FLY
THROUGH THE SKY?
ON A HOT AIR BALLOON
WITH CLOUDS
ROLLING BY?**

Curious Dreamer,
WILL YOU SWING,
WILL YOU GLIDE?
AND SWOOSH TO THE GROUND
DOWN A RAINBOW SLIDE?

Curious Dreamer,
SNUGGLE IN TIGHT,
WITH YOUR BLANKET,
A HUG, AND A SWEET KISS
Good Night!

The Goodnight Train

June Sobel

Illustrated by Laura Huliska-Beith

To the memory of Clara Sobel,
who loved the world of books.
—J. S.

For Amelie, the newlywed, and Betty,
the newly graduated. Here's to new love,
new adventures, and more naps.
—L. H. B.

The Goodnight Train gets set to roll.
It's being shined and filled with coal.

75

Wash the cars off with a hose.
Scrub the engine's dirty nose.

Scrub-a-dub! Scrub-a-dub! Toot! Toot!

All aboard! The sun is down.
The Goodnight Train is leaving town.

78

Find your sleepers! Grab your teddy.
Climb right up! Your bed is ready!

"All tucked in," the porter cries.
"Pillows fluffed. Now close your eyes."

WHOO

Wheels are turning. Smoke drifts high, painting clouds up in the sky.

Huff-a-puff-a! Huff-a-puff-a!

Slumber, lumber up the hill.
Cars climb slowly up until . . .

Roll the corner, rock the curve.
Blankets bounce with every swerve.

Rock-a, rock-a, rock-a, rock-a—

Shhhhhhhhhhh!
Shhhhhhhhhhh!

Fly through a tunnel black as ink—
in and out before you blink.

Catch that freight train whizzing past!
The Goodnight Train is moving fast!

Cars sway on the wooden track.
Wheels go click. Wheels go clack.

Glide across a plain so flat.
Gently toss this way and that.

CLICKETY - CLACK!

CLICKETY - CLACK!

CLICKETY - CLACK!

Curl through farms of fuzzy sheep.
The sleepy train slows to a creep.

Pushing toward the station's light,
cars crawl on with all their might.

Chug...chug...Chug!

"Sweet dreams ahead," the porter sighs.
The tired train can close its eyes.

Home at last, tucked in and snug,
the engine snores a final "Chug!"

Hush-a, hush-a, hush-a, hush-a— *Sleeeeeeeeep!*

Good night, train.
Good night.

Alligator

Old bull of the waters,
old dinosaur cousin,
with scales by the hundreds
and teeth by the dozen,

old singer of swamplands,
old slithery swimmer,
what do you dream of
when fireflies glimmer?

Can you remember
the folktales of old
when you breathed fire
and guarded the gold,

and stole lovely ladies
and captured their kings,
and flew over mountains
on magical wings?

Old bull of the waters,
how can you know
that men made you a dragon,
in dreams, long ago?

by Maxine Kumin
illustrated by Pamela Zagarenski

No Sleep for the Sheep!

WRITTEN BY **Karen Beaumont**

ILLUSTRATED BY **Jackie Urbanovic**

Sweet dreams and lots of love to my dear friends
Cyndi and Patrick
— K.B.

For my brother Tony and my sister-in-law Barb,
with love
— J.U.

In the big red barn on the farm, on the farm,
in the big red barn on the farm . . .

A sheep fell asleep in the big red barn,
in the big red barn on the farm.

Then there came a loud **QUACK**
at the door, at the door,
and the sheep couldn't sleep any more.

"Go to sleep!" said the sheep
to the duck at the door.
"And please don't **QUACK** any more!"

"**QUACK!**" said the duck in the barn.
"Shhh! Not a peep! Go to sleep!" said the sheep
in the big red barn on the farm.

Soon the duck and the sheep fell fast asleep
in the big red barn on the farm.

Then there came a loud **BAAA**
at the door, at the door,
and the sheep couldn't sleep any more.

"Go to sleep!" said the sheep
to the goat at the door.
"And please don't BAAA any more!"

"BAAA!" said the goat in the barn.
"Shhh! Not a peep! Go to sleep!" said the sheep
in the big red barn on the farm.

Soon the goat and the sheep fell fast asleep
in the big red barn on the farm.

Then there came a loud

OINK

at the door, at the door,
and the sheep couldn't sleep any more.

"Go to sleep!" said the sheep
to the pig at the door.
"And please don't **OINK** any more!"

"**OINK!**" said the pig in the barn.
"Shhh! Not a peep! Go to sleep!" said the sheep
in the big red barn on the farm.

Soon the pig and the sheep fell fast asleep
in the big red barn on the farm.

Then there came a loud

MOO

at the door, at the door,
and the sheep couldn't sleep any more.

"Go to sleep!" said the sheep
to the cow at the door.
"And please don't MOO any more!"

"MOO!" said the cow in the barn.
"Shhh! Not a peep! Go to sleep!" said the sheep
in the big red barn on the farm.

Soon the cow and the sheep fell fast asleep
in the big red barn on the farm.

Then there came a loud

NEIGHHHH

at the door, at the door,
and the sheep couldn't sleep any more.

"Go to sleep!" said the sheep
to the horse at the door.
"And please don't NEIGH any more!"

"**NEIGH!**" said the horse in the barn.

"Shhh! Not a peep! Go to sleep!" said the sheep
in the big red barn on the farm.

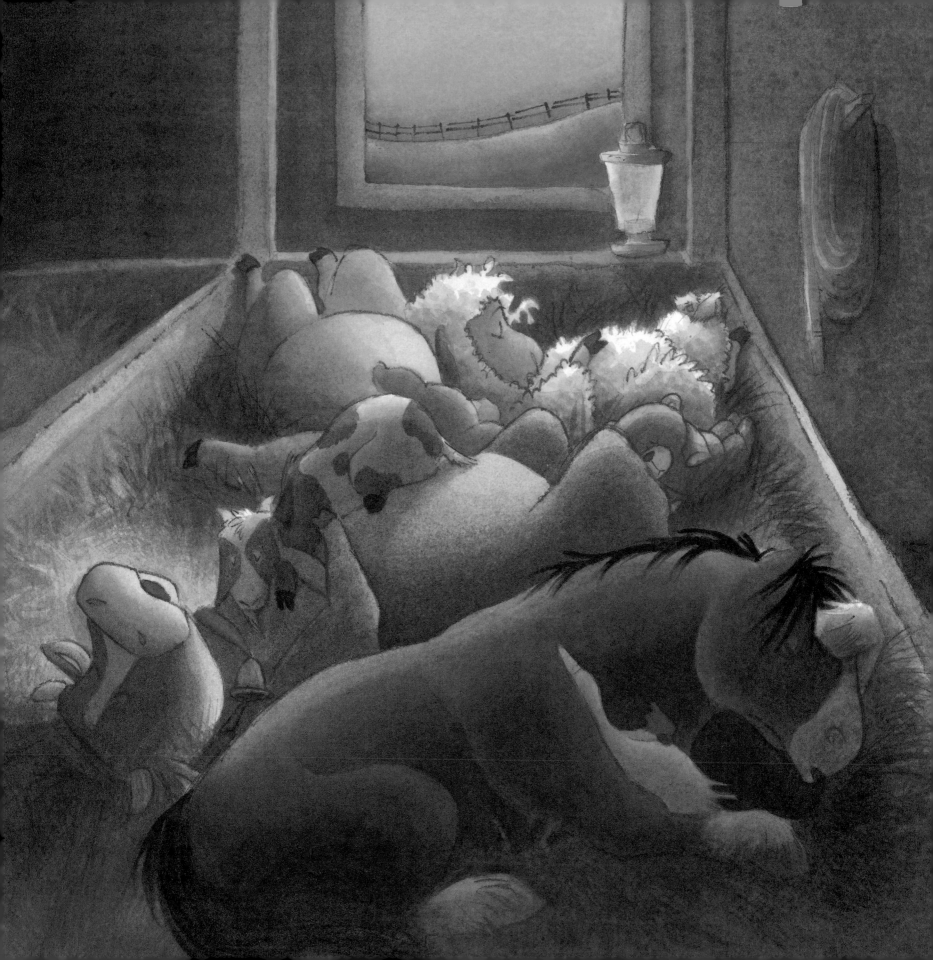

Soon the horse and the sheep fell fast asleep
in the big red barn on the farm.

In a deep, deep sleep in the big red barn,
in the big red barn on the farm . . .

Then . . .

DOODLE-DOO

"Wake up, all of you!
Hey, Sheep! That means you, too!"

But the sheep slept right on through . . .
through the neighs and the moos
and the cock-a-doodle-doos
in the big red barn on the farm.

YOUNG MOTH

Go forth,
Young Moth.
It takes strength
to lift up and stay aloft
with wings so soft.
Once in flight,
be swift,
or drift all night.
Return to earth
when lights go off.
Sleep tight,
Young Moth.

by Calef Brown

THE QUIET BOOK

By Deborah Underwood   Illustrated by Renata Liwska

For Sarah, with love —D.U.

To my editor Kate, for her support and trust —R.L.

There are many kinds of quiet:

First one awake quiet

Jelly side down quiet

Don't scare the robin quiet

Others telling secrets quiet

Coloring in the lines quiet

Thinking of a good reason you were
drawing on the wall quiet

Hide-and-seek quiet

Last one to get picked up from school quiet

Swimming underwater quiet

153

Pretending you're invisible quiet

Lollipop quiet

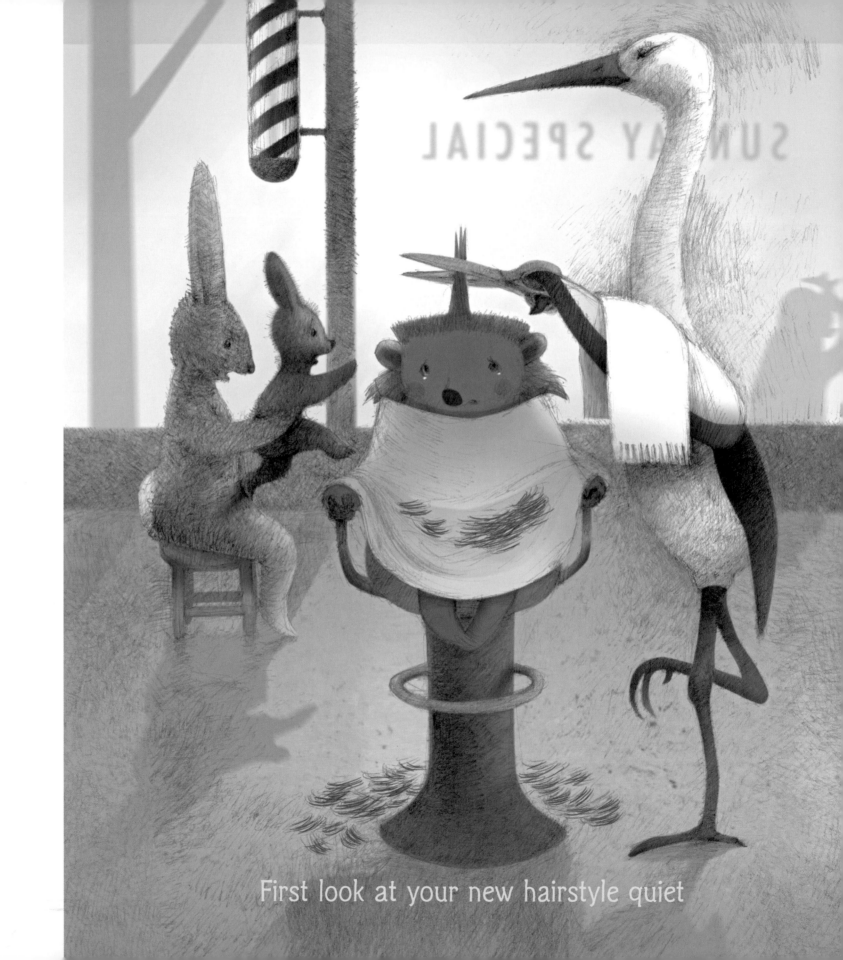

First look at your new hairstyle quiet

Sleeping sister quiet

Right before you yell "SURPRISE!" quiet

Making a wish quiet

Top of the roller coaster quiet

Best friends don't need to talk quiet

Surprise visit from Aunt Tillie quiet

Do iguanas bite? quiet

Before the concert starts quiet

Trying not to hiccup quiet

First snowfall quiet

Car ride at night quiet

Too many bubbles quiet

Story time quiet

Tucking in Teddy quiet

Bedtime kiss quiet

"What flashlight?" quiet

Sound asleep quiet

Lullaby

Tree sighs softly
as the birds patter about
her heavy old branches,
settling down,
tucking their heads
beneath their wings.

She waits until dusk
has shadowed her leaves,
and when she's sure
she's heard that last
soft cheep,

she rocks her birds to sleep.

by Kristine O'Connell George
illustrated by Kate Kiesler

Tell Me Something Happy Before I Go to Sleep

JOYCE DUNBAR • DEBI GLIORI

Willa was tired,
so Willa went to bed.

She lay with her pillow this way . . .
and that way . . . and another way.
But Willa couldn't sleep.

"Willoughby," called Willa. "Are you there?"

"Yes," answered Willoughby. "I'm here."

"I can't sleep," said Willa.

"Why can't you sleep?" asked Willoughby.

"I'm afraid," said Willa.

"What are you afraid of?" asked Willoughby.

"I'm afraid that I might have a bad dream," said Willa.

"Think of something happy, then you won't have a bad dream," said Willoughby.

So Willa tried to think of something happy,
but she couldn't.

"Willoughby," called Willa. "Are you still there?"

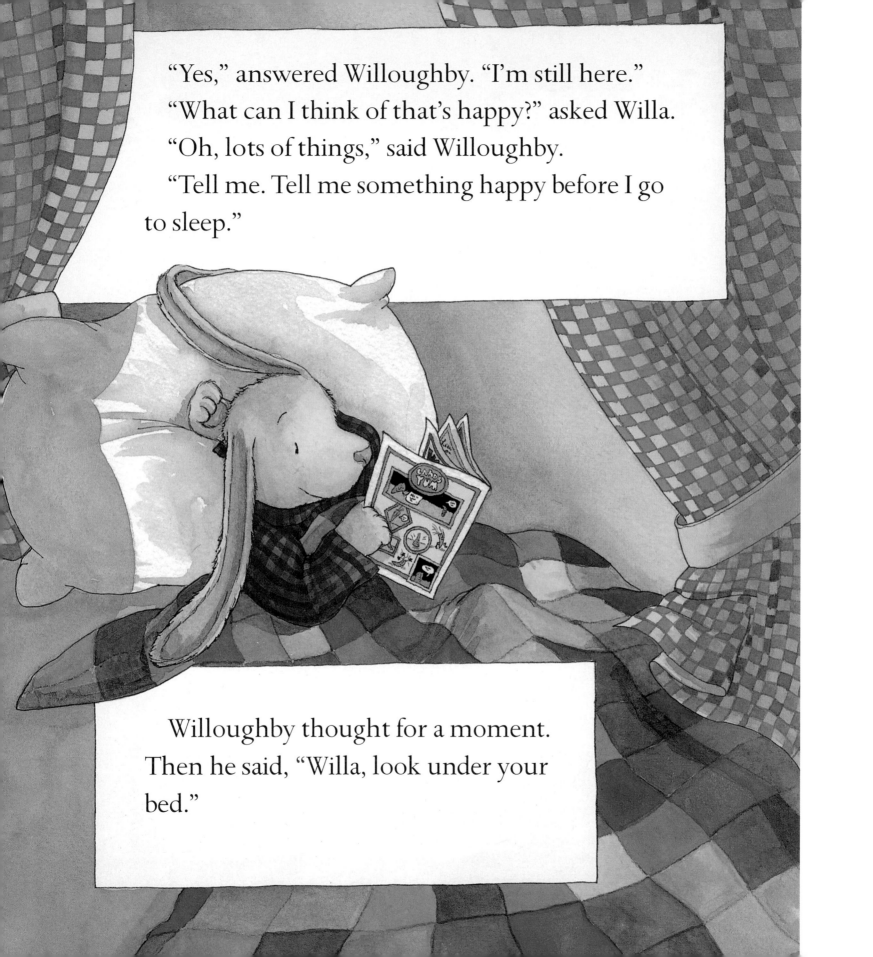

"Yes," answered Willoughby. "I'm still here."

"What can I think of that's happy?" asked Willa.

"Oh, lots of things," said Willoughby.

"Tell me. Tell me something happy before I go to sleep."

Willoughby thought for a moment. Then he said, "Willa, look under your bed."

So Willa leaned over and looked under her bed.
"What do you see?" asked Willoughby.
"I see my chicken slippers," said Willa.
"That's right," said Willoughby.

"And do you know what your chicken slippers are doing?"

"No," said Willa. "I don't."

"They are waiting, just waiting, for nobody's feet but yours."

"Good," said Willa. "That's happy. What else?"

"What do you see on the chair?" asked Willoughby.

"I see my blue-and-white jumpsuit," said Willa.

"Do you know what your jumpsuit is doing?" asked Willoughby.

"No," said Willa. "I don't."

"It is longing, just longing, for tomorrow, when you will jump out of bed and put it on."

"Good," said Willa. "That's happy. What else?"

Willoughby picked Willa up in his arms and padded softly downstairs to the kitchen. He opened the pantry door.

"What do you see on the shelves?" asked Willoughby.

"I see bread and honey and oats and milk and apples," said Willa.

"That's right," said Willoughby, "all waiting to be made into breakfast, for you and me to share."

"Oh good," said Willa. "That's happy. What else?"

Willoughby carried Willa into the living room and switched on the lamp.

"What do you see in the corner?" asked Willoughby.

"I see my basket full of toys," said Willa.

"What do you think they are doing?" asked Willoughby.

"I don't know," said Willa.

"They are dreaming, dreaming of tomorrow, and the games you are going to play."

"That's very happy," said Willa. "What else?"

Willoughby carried Willa to the window and opened the curtains wide.

"What do you see in the darkness?" asked Willoughby.

"I see only the night," said Willa.

"What do you think the night is doing?" asked Willoughby.

"I don't know," said Willa.

"The night is waiting, waiting for the morning, which is on its way round the world."

"That's happy," said Willa.

"The morning is waiting, too," said Willoughby.

"What for?" asked Willa.

"Oh, lots of things," said Willoughby.

"What things?" asked Willa.

"For grass to grow, flowers to bloom, and leaves to flutter. For clouds to float, wind to blow, and sun to shine. For birds to fly, bees to buzz, and ducks to quack."

"That's a lot of happy things," said Willa.

"There's just one sad thing," said Willoughby.

"What's that?" asked Willa.

"The morning is waiting for you, too. It's waiting to wake you up."

"But I'm awake already," said Willa.

"That's why it's sad," said Willoughby. "The morning likes waking you up. That's what makes the morning happy."

"Willoughby," said Willa.

"What is it?" asked Willoughby.

"I'm tired."

So Willoughby carried Willa back to bed.

"What do you see in your bed?" asked Willoughby.

"I see my bear," said Willa.

"What do you think he is doing?" asked Willoughby.

"Waiting for me to snuggle up with him," said Willa.

"That's right," said Willoughby, "waiting especially for you."

"And when the morning comes and wakes me up, will you still be here?" asked Willa.

"I'll still be here," said Willoughby.

"Good," said Willa. "That's the happiest thing of all!"

"Good night, Willa."

But Willa didn't answer. She was sound asleep.

I Hold Thee, My Baby

HAWAII, TRADITIONAL

I hold thee, my baby,
I hold thee, my baby.
I rock thee landwards.
I rock thee seawards.
My own child,
Rest.

Illustrated by
Kate Kiesler

*For Ayden—welcome to
the family!*

Gideon

Olivier Dunrea

This is Gideon.

Gideon is a small, ruddy gosling
who likes to play. All day.

Gideon marches to the piggery.

He plays chase-the-piglet.

Gideon dashes to the henhouse.

He plays find-the-eggs.

"Gideon, time for your nap," his mother calls.

"No nap! I'm playing!"

Gideon hops to the field.

He plays tag-the-mole.

Gideon chases butterflies in the meadow.

He sneaks behind a beetle on a rock.

"Gideon, time for your nap," his mother calls.

"No nap! I'm playing!"

Gideon scurries to the pond.

He splashes with the ducklings.

Gideon scoots to the beehives.

He listens to the bees buzzing inside the hive.

"Gideon, time for your nap," his mother calls.

"No nap! I'm playing!"

Gideon scampers to the sheep house.

He bounces on the back of the ewe.

Gideon leaps over a green frog.

He plays quietly with a small turtle.

Gideon wanders to the field.

He scrambles to the top of the haystack.

"Gideon, time for your nap," his mother calls.

Gideon doesn't answer.

Gideon is a small, ruddy gosling
who likes to play . . . almost all day.
Shhh . . .

when
stars
make
wishes
they
wish
they
could
drink
the
raindrops
and
never
fall
leaving
their
last
flash
of
light
for
the
earth
they
shine
upon

by Dana Jensen
illustrated by Tricia Tusa

Bedtime Bunnies

WORDS AND PICTURES BY **Wendy Watson**

For Elizabeth

Bedtime, Bunnies!

Skip

Scurry

Scamper

Hop

249

Sip   Slurp   Guzzle   Gulp

Squirt　Scrub　Splutter　Spit

Swish

Slosh

Bubble

Splash

Pop

Zip

Button   Snap

Giggle Wiggle

Snuggle Squeeze

Climb Bounce Jump Thump

Dearie   Darling

Cuddle Hug

Quiet

Shush

Hush

Shhh

Good night, bunnies.

With the ember end
of my long marshmallow stick,
I draw on the dark.

by Bob Raczka
illustrated by Peter H. Reynolds

Meet the Authors and Illustrators

AUDREY WOOD AND DON WOOD

Audrey Wood is the author of more than thirty popular children's books, including *Piggies,* an ALA Notable Children's Book, *Silly Sally,* and *Heckedy Peg.* She lives with her husband, Don, in Hawaii.

Don Wood first illustrated a picture book for his wife, Audrey, and since then has illustrated several superb children's books, including *Piggies, Heckedy Peg,* and *Piggy Pie Po,* all written by Audrey Wood.

You can learn more about the Woods and their other wonderful books at www.audreywood.com.

EILEEN CHRISTELOW

Eileen Christelow has written and illustrated many fun and funny picture books, including the popular Five Little Monkeys series, *Vote!,* and *Letters from a Desperate Dog.* She and her husband, Ahren, live in Vermont.

For more information about Five Little Monkeys, fun activities, information on how illustrations are created, and comic strips, visit www.christelow.com and www.fivelittlemonkeys.com.

  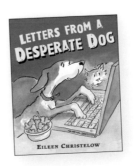 

JUNE SOBEL AND LAURA HULISKA-BEITH

JUNE SOBEL is also the author of several wonderful picture books, including *The Goodnight Train, B Is for Bulldozer,* and *Shiver Me Letters*. She lives with her husband and son in Westlake Village, California. Visit her website at www.junesobel.com.

LAURA HULISKA-BEITH has illustrated many fantastic books for children, including *The Recess Queen* by Alexis O'Neill, *Ten Little Lady Bugs* by Melanie Gerth, and her own *The Book of Bad Ideas.* She lives with her husband and three dogs in Kansas City, Missouri. Visit her at www.laurahuliskabeith.com.

KAREN BEAUMONT

KAREN BEAUMONT is the author of numerous celebrated picture books, including the New York Times bestseller *I Ain't Gonna Paint No More!,* illustrated by David Catrow, and the critically acclaimed *Move Over, Rover!,* illustrated by Jane Dyer. She lives in California. For more information, visit www.karenbeaumont.com.

   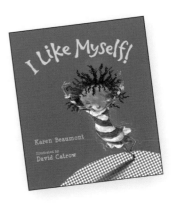

DEBORAH UNDERWOOD AND RENATA LIWSKA

DEBORAH UNDERWOOD is the author of many not so quiet books, including *Pirate Mom,* illustrated by Stephen Gilpin, *Granny Gomez and Jigsaw,* illustrated by Scott Magoon, and, of course, *The Loud Book!,* illustrated by Renata Liwska. She lives in San Francisco and loves "cat sleeping on your stomach quiet" and "smelling lilacs quiet." Find out more about her at www.deborahunderwoodbooks.com.

RENATA LIWSKA's favorite kind of quiet is "drawing a picture book quiet." She also collaborated with Deborah Underwood on *The Loud Book!* and *The Christmas Quiet Book,* and is the author and illustrator of several other books, including *Little Panda.* She lives in Calgary, Canada, with her husband, Mike. Visit her online at www.renataliwska.com.

JOYCE DUNBAR AND DEBI GLIORI

JOYCE DUNBAR has written more than fifty books for children, including *Tell Me What It's Like to Be Big* and *The Very Small,* both illustrated by Debi Gliori. Her books have been translated into several languages. Dunbar lives in Norwich, England, with her cat, Minnie Ha-Ha. Find out more about her work at www.joycedunbar.com.

DEBI GLIORI has illustrated many beloved picture books, including Joyce Dunbar's *Tell Me What It's Like to Be Big,* as well as her own *No Matter What* and *Penguin Post.* She lives near Edinburgh, Scotland. Visit her at www.debglioribooks.com.

OLIVIER DUNREA

OLIVER DUNREA is the award-winning creator of the best-selling Gossie & Friends books and the author and illustrator of more than fifty children's books. He lives, writes, and paints in a tiny remote village in the Catskill Mountains in upstate New York. Visit his website at www.olivierdunrea.com.

  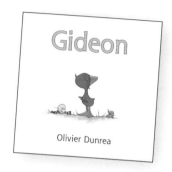

WENDY WATSON

WENDY WATSON has written and illustrated more than twenty picture books, including *Bedtime Bunnies* and *Boo! It's Halloween,* and has illustrated eighty more by other authors. A longtime Vermont resident, she now divides her time between Phoenix, Arizona, and Cape Cod, Massachusetts. Find out more at www.wendy-watson.com.

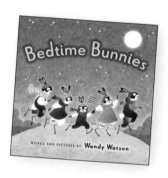  

JOYCE SIDMAN AND RICK ALLEN

JOYCE SIDMAN is the award-winning poet of *Song of the Water Boatman*, *Red Sings from Treetops*, and *Dark Emperor and Other Poems of the Night,* a Newbery Honor book. She has won both the Lee Bennet Hopkins Award and Bank Street's Claudia Lewis Award for her poetry. She lives in Wayzata, Minnesota.

RICK ALLEN made his picture book debut with *Dark Emperor and Other Poems of the Night.* A master printmaker, he produces original linoleum cuts, curious wood engravings, eccentric broadsheets, and other printed ephemerae at the Kenspeckle Letterpress in Duluth, Minnesota. Explore his work at www.kenspeckleletterpress.com.

H. A. AND MARGRET REY

Hans Augusto Rey and Margret Rey escaped Nazi-occupied Paris in 1940 by bicycle, carrying the manuscript for the first book about Curious George. They came to live in the United States, and *Curious George* was published in 1941. You can learn more about the Reys and Curious George, and access games, activities, downloads, and PBS television shows at www.curiousgeorge.com.

MAXINE KUMIN AND PAMELA ZAGARENSKI

Maxine Kumin is the author of sixteen books of poetry and twenty children's books. She has served as poet laureate of both New Hampshire and the United States, and is the recipient of many awards, most notably the Pulitzer Prize in 1973 for her book of poetry, *Up Country.* She lives with her husband, Victor, in New Hampshire. Visit her at www.maxinekumin.com.

Pamela Zagarenski is a Caldecott Honor winner and has illustrated many beautiful books, including *Red Sings from Treetops* and *What Color Is It?* She divides her time between Stonington, Connecticut, and Prince Edward Island.

CALEF BROWN

Calef Brown is an artist and writer whose illustrations have appeared in many magazines and newspapers, and his paintings have been exhibited in N.Y., L.A., S.F., and other places without fancy initials, such as Osaka and Rome. His books for Houghton Mifflin Harcourt include the successful *Polkabats and Octopus Slacks, Dutch Sneakers and Flea Keepers,* and *Flamingos on the Roof.* He lives in Maine, and you can learn more about his books, poetry, and artwork at www.calefbrown.com.

KRISTINE O'CONNELL GEORGE AND KATE KIESLER

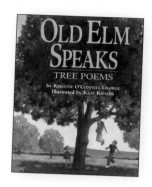

KRISTINE O'CONNELL GEORGE's many volumes of poetry for children have received numerous honors, including the Lee Bennett Hopkins Poetry Award, the International Reading Association / Lee Bennett Promising Poet Award, the Myra Cohn Livingston Poetry Award, and the Claudia Lewis Poetry Award. To find out more about Kristine O'Connell George's books, and to find activities for teachers and children and read-aloud audio clips, visit www.kristinegeorge.com.

KATE KIESLER is a fine artist and illustrator who has created art for more than twenty books for children, including *Crab Moon* by Ruth Horowitz and *The Great Frog Race* by Kristine O'Connell George. She lives in Colorado, the landscape of which inspires much of her painting. Visit her at www.katekieslerfineart.com.

DANA JENSEN AND TRICIA TUSA

DANA JENSEN both writes and teaches poetry to children. *A Meal of the Stars* is his debut collection.

TRICIA TUSA has illustrated more than forty children's books, including the *New York Times* best-selling *The Sandwich Swap* by Queen Rania of Jordan Al Abdullah, and *The Magic Hat* by Mem Fox, which was chosen as an IRA-CBC Children's Choice. She has her master's in art therapy, and lives with her family in northern New Mexico.

BOB RACZKA AND PETER REYNOLDS

BOB RACZKA lives with his wife, sons, daughter, and dog, Rufus, in Glen Ellyn, Illinois. He is the author of several children's books, but *Guyku* is his first with Houghton Mifflin Harcourt. Raczka's favorite guy things include art, baseball, books, golf, grilling, and poetry. Visit him at www.bobraczka.com.

PETER H. REYNOLDS is a *New York Times* best-selling illustrator who has created many acclaimed books for children, including *The Dot, Ish,* and *The North Star.* His Massachusetts bookstore, The Blue Bunny, and his company, FableVision, are dedicated to sharing "stories that matter, stories that move." To access blogs, news, tips for writers, and artwork, visit www.peterhreynolds.com.

Published in the United States by HMH Books, an imprint of Houghton Mifflin Harcourt Publishing Company.

www.hmhbooks.com

ISBN 978-0-547-85786-2

Manufactured in China
LEO 10 9 8 7 6 5 4 3 2 1
4500350806